Printed in the United States of America   COM-UNI
                    First Edition   10 9 8 7 6 5 4 3 2 1
ISBN 0-316-73382-2

ARTHUR'S
Jelly Beans

by Marc Brown

LITTLE, BROWN AND COMPANY
New York ❧ An AOL Time Warner Company

Everyone lined up and poured out their jelly beans.
Muffy walked down the line counting.
"Fern . . . seven. The Brain . . . six. Three for you,
Binky . . . and nine for Francine."
Then she came to Arthur.

Muffy handed Arthur the big chocolate egg.
"I hope you'll all help me eat this," Arthur said.
"Really?" said Buster.
"Of course!" said Arthur. "I could never finish it.
After all . . . "

"You know how slow I am!"